Megan McDonald

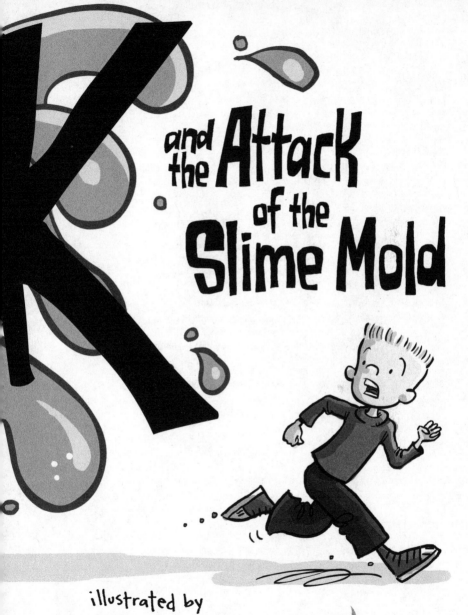

K and the Attack of the Slime Mold

illustrated by

Peter H. Reynolds

CANDLEWICK PRESS

Text copyright © 2016 by Megan McDonald
Illustrations copyright © 2016 by Peter H. Reynolds
Stink®. Stink is a registered trademark of Candlewick Press, Inc.

First paperback edition 2017

Library of Congress Catalog Card Number 2015937112
ISBN 978-0-7636-5554-9 (hardcover)
ISBN 978-0-7636-5940-0 (paperback)

17 18 19 20 21 BVG 10 9 8 7 6 5 4 3 2

Printed in Berryville, VA, U.S.A.

This book was typeset in Stone Informal and Judy Moody.
The illustrations were created digitally.

Candlewick Press
99 Dover Street
Somerville, Massachusetts 02144

visit us at www.candlewick.com

for Ginger
M. M.

To Jess Brallier
P. H. R.

CONTENTS

The Glob.............................1

Slime Mold Saturday...............13

Mr. McGoo Sees the World! 31

Sneeze of Doom................... 57

Frankenslime 73

The Incredible Shrinking Slime.... 87

McGoo Two 107

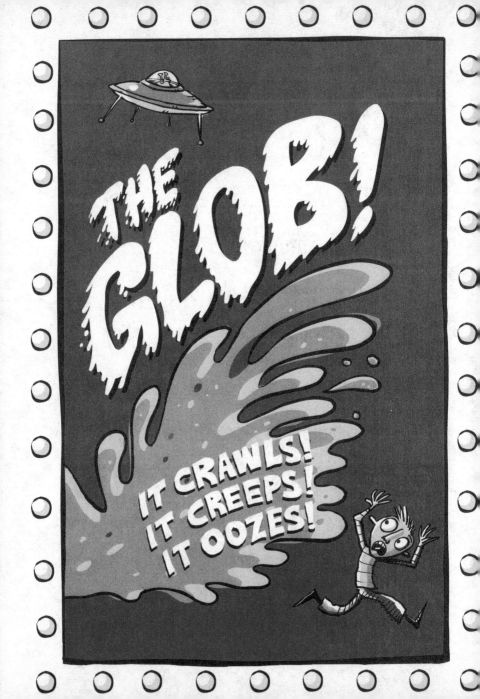

*G*lip!

 Glop!

  Gloop!

 "It crawls! It creeps! It oozes! It comes from outer space!"

 "First it was some sort of blob stuck to his hand. Then it landed on his head. It kept getting bigger and bigger and BIGGER. And then, all of a sudden, he just sort of . . . disappeared!"

"What do you mean . . . disappeared?"

"The thing . . . it ATE him. Right before my eyes."

"Was it a monster?"

"It was worse than a monster. It was THE GLOB!"

"AAAAAGGGHHH!"

"Aaagh!" Stink screamed. He pulled his T-shirt up over his eyes so he would not have to look at the movie screen. Judy jumped. Her popcorn went flying all over the backseat of the car.

In the front seat, Mom and Dad chuckled.

"Whose brainy idea was it to come to the drive-in movies, anyway?" Stink said, with a shiver in his voice.

"Yours," said Mom, Dad, and Judy at the same time.

"Well, I thought it would be cool to get to sit in the car and watch a movie. Outside. Under the stars."

The Stardust, an old drive-in movie theater like the kind that had been around when Mom and Dad were kids, had just reopened in Frog Neck Lake.

"It *is* cool," said Judy.

"And dark," said Stink. "And a little scary."

"It's dark at the inside movies, too," Judy pointed out. "Besides, it's the Friday Night Freak Fest, Stink. You wanted to see an old monster movie. It's *supposed* to be freaky."

Stink couldn't bear to look at the screen. At the same time, he couldn't bear *not* to look. He peeked out over the top of his T-shirt. A screaming crowd came running out of a diner.

The Glob was oozing down the street.

"It's taking over the whole town!"

"Nothing will stop it, Doctor! It's the most horrible thing I've ever seen!"

Stink screamed again. He turned and looked at Judy with saucer eyes. "What if the Glob eats the whole town?"

"It's not real, Stink, remember? Think of it like a giant glob of Jell-O. Jell-O's not scary, is it?"

Stink leaned in and stuck his head between Mom and Dad. "More popcorn, please." Mom passed the bag back to Stink.

"We're going to have to find the biggest plane we can get our hands on and take this thing to the Arctic, where it'll freeze for good."

"Will that work?"

"We have to do something before it wipes out the whole town."

Stink and Judy watched wide-eyed until the end. "Good thing they found a plane big enough to take the Glob to the North Pole and freeze it," said Stink.

"Poor Santa," said Judy.

"Mom? Dad? Can we stay for the second show?" Stink asked. "It's *Son of Glob*."

"Stink," said Mom, "you covered your eyes for half the movie."

"So?"

"So," said Dad, "I think we've had enough glob for one night. Besides, we have to get you home to bed. Tomorrow you have Saturday Science Club, Stink."

On the way home, Stink could not get the Glob out of his head. When they turned onto Croaker Road, he imagined it following them, oozing down the street, up the sidewalk to his front door, and into his very own house.

That's when he remembered something truly terrifying. He remembered
the experiment they were going to be
doing tomorrow in Saturday Science
Club.

AAAAAGGGHHH!

That night, Stink dreamed of oozy-goozy, blobby-globby goo taking over the earth. When he woke up, he tried to erase it from his mind like chalk from an old blackboard. But even his oatmeal looked like the Attack of the Glob Monster.

All the way to Saturday Science Club, Stink could not stop thinking of globby things. Blobs. Globs. Brains. Oozy-woozy slime. Jiggly-wiggly Jell-O. When he got to the Discovery Center, someone was waiting for him outside the front door. That someone was . . .

Riley Rottenberger.

Sometimes Riley Rottenberger acted rotten. Stink hoped today was not one of those times.

Riley waved a braid at him and grinned, showing off a missing tooth. "Stink! Over here! Are you ready for Slime Mold Saturday?"

14

"I guess," said Stink.

"You don't sound very excited," said Riley. "What happened? We've been waiting for this since way back when we were doing Weather."

Stink did not want to tell Riley that he was spooked by an old-timey blob movie. So he tried to smile and fake it. "Are you kidding? I'm in. C'mon. Let's get slimed!"

"It's not just slime, Stink. It's slime *mold*."

Riley was already an expert in all things slime mold. Her mom was head of Saturday Science Club. Riley liked to use big words. Stink hoped she was not going to act show-offy all day.

"So what exactly is slime mold, anyway? Animal, vegetable, or mineral?"

"No, no, and no. Slime mold is not really a plant, and it's not really an animal. It's different from the mold that grows on old bread. Slime mold is a one-celled organism. Kind of like an amoeba."

"But it looks like dog vomit, right?" Stink grinned. "And smells like a corpse flower?"

"It *does* look like dog vomit," said Riley, "but it can also look like brains. Or mucus."

"Sweet!" said Stink. "Anything that looks like mucus is A-okay with me. As long as it doesn't grow as big as the Glob and attack us."

Mrs. Rottenberger asked everyone to take a seat. Riley slipped into the chair next to Stink.

Riley's mom drew blobs all over the board. She used big words like *amoeba* and *Protista*. She put pictures of slime molds on the screen. Some looked like pink spiderwebs. Some looked like red-hot candies. Some looked like exploding pretzels. They all looked like dog puke.

Stink raised his hand. "So a slime mold is a blob of goo, but it has no brains and no feet?" he asked Riley's mom. "And it can grow and grow and move around like crazy?"

Mrs. Rottenberger nodded and said, "That's right. If a slime mold is hungry, it can even join up with other slime molds. Then they move together like one big sausage."

"A walking sausage. That's a good one," said Stink.

"Has anybody seen the movie *The Glob*?" asked Mrs. Rottenberger.

Stink could not believe his ears. He put his hand up.

Riley pulled his arm down. "You did not," she said.

"Yah-huh." Stink waved his hand

again. He practically jumped out of his seat.

"Stink," said Mrs. Rottenberger, calling on him.

"I saw it just last night. At the drive-in movie theater."

"Whoa," said Riley. "Weren't you scared? I was scared of Oogie Boogie, that bogeyman in *The Nightmare Before Christmas*."

"Me?" asked Stink. "No way." He sat up taller and squared his shoulders, trying to look his bravest.

Riley's mom went on. "Did you know,

the idea for the *Glob* movie came from slime molds?"

It did?

"In real life, some slime molds can grow to be as big as three feet across."

"And take over the planet," said Stink.

"Only in the movies," said Mrs. R., smiling.

Phew.

"Your mom is the coolest," Stink whispered to Riley.

"Look who's talking," said Riley. "Your mom dressed up like a zombie lunch lady once!"

"Oh, yeah," Stink said, sniggering.

"Listen up, everybody," said Mrs. Rottenberger. "Today, we are going to grow our own slime mold."

"For real?" asked Stink. "We'll be like Dr. Finkelstein, that mad-scientist guy in *The Nightmare Before Christmas*."

Riley shuddered. "He gives me the creeps!"

"Not me," said Stink. "I love how he can pop open his head and scratch his brain when he's thinking."

"Shh," said Riley, pointing to her mom.

"Everybody gets a starter kit," said Mrs. R. "I'll help you set up the experiment in class, and then you can take your mold home and watch it grow."

Mrs. Rottenberger passed out small glass petri dishes and instructions. Stink could not wait. He tugged on a pair of gloves. He lined the bottom of his small glass dish with a wet paper towel. Then, he oh-so-carefully set the slime-mold sample in the dish. Next, he placed one-two-three oat flakes next to the slime-mold starter.

While Mrs. Rottenberger helped the other kids set up their experiments, Stink stared at his dish. He blinked. He watched. He waited. He blinked some more.

Nothing happened.

Stink stuck his hand in the air. "When will it be ready to take over the planet?" he asked. "Or at least my sister's room?"

Everybody cracked up. "I'm afraid it's going to be a while," said Riley's mom.

Stink peered at his tiny blob. "I made you with my own hands," he cackled in a mad-scientist voice *à la* Dr. Finkelstein.

"Okay, junior scientists," said Mrs. R. "When you're ready, put your slime mold dish in a shoe box. Take it home and keep it in a warm, dark place. But not too warm—you don't want it to dry out."

Stink peered down at the petri dish in his shoe box. It was hard to believe that one tiny dab of goo could grow into a giant glob.

"Check on your mold in ten or twelve hours. Write down any changes you notice. Next week we'll be building solar ovens to cook s'mores. We can look over your slime-mold journals again in two weeks. Class is over for today."

"Two weeks?" said Stink. "By then, I could be blob food!"

"I can't believe Science Club is over already," said Riley. "Rats."

"Slime flies when you're having fun," said Stink.

On Sunday, Stink woke up before Mom and Dad. Before Judy. He even woke up before Mouse or Toady or Astro. He did not read his *Big Head Book of Sharks*. He did not draw Stink Frog comics.

He ran over to his closet and pulled out the shoe box so he could check on his slime mold. Ooh. Sick-awesome! The slime mold was growing. The slime mold was pulsing. The slime mold was on the move. It looked like science fiction. It looked like Horta, a stinky blob in Dad's favorite episode of *Star Trek.*

Stink grabbed his notebook. He wrote stuff down just like Captain Kirk in *Star Trek:*

CAPTAIN'S LOG: SLIME DATE 3196.1
1ST day of slime tracking.
Gob of goo starting to grow.
Has made contact with oatmeal.
Slimed three oats!

Stink's heart skipped a beat. He had a new pet! Maybe it didn't have fur like Astro or say "Ribbet" like Toady. Maybe it wasn't the sugar glider he'd always wanted, but it was still way cool!

Stink had to give his new pet a name.

CAPTAIN'S LOG: SLIMEDATE 3196.2

~~Googol~~

~~Goosebump~~

~~The Glob, Junior~~

~~Jellybelly~~

~~Sluggo~~

Mr. McGoo!! ← YES! THAT'S IT!

Eureka! Stink ran to tell Judy. "Knock, knock," he called.

"Go away. I'm sleeping," said his sister, hiding her book under the covers.

"No, you're not. You're reading mini-mysteries," said Stink.

"I'm trying to solve the mini-mystery of why you're waking me up so early."

"Come see Mr. McGoo!" said Stink.

"Mr. Mc*Who*?" Judy asked. She crawled out of bed. Stink dragged her over into his room. Judy peered into the glass dish. "Gross. It looks like snot."

"Does *snot*," said Stink. "It looks like

the inside of a jellyfish. Or the inside of a brain! Isn't it the coolest?"

"If you say so," said Judy. "Now can I go back to bed?"

Stink showed Mom and Dad. "And in a week or two, it'll look like dog vomit!" Stink told them.

Mom made a face and stuck out her tongue.

"No dog vomit before breakfast, Stink," Dad said, shooing him out of the room.

"Poor McGoo," said Stink. "Nobody gets you like I do."

✳ ✳ ✳

Under Stink's watchful eye, Mr. McGoo
continued to grow.

CAPTAIN'S LOG: SLIME DATE 3196.4
Mission Possible: Get slime mold
to keep growing.
Fed one Cheerio, one rice puff.
Slime mold in pursuit of Cheerio.
Good call, McGoo!

That gob of goo grew and grew and grew.

CAPTAIN'S LOG: SLIME DATE 3196.7
Amazing Observation #1:
Mr. McGoo size of silver dollar.

I ♥

CAPTAIN'S LOG: SLIME DATE 3196.13
AO#2: Mr. McGoo size of silver-dollar pancake!
(AMAZING OBSERVATION)

CAPTAIN'S LOG: SLIME DATE 3196.17
AO#3: Mr. McGoo almost size of for-real pancake!

At last it was time. Time to share Mr. McGoo with the world!

Stink put his slime mold back in the shoe box and took Mr. McGoo on a tour of the neighborhood. He showed Mr. McGoo the crack in the pavement that looked like a great white shark. He showed Mr. McGoo the rock where a blue-tailed skink sunned itself. He showed Mr. McGoo the best mulberry tree for collecting monkey balls—wrinkled fruit that looks like green brains.

"And this," he told Mr. McGoo, "is the exact spot where I found a moon rock one time. No lie. Now it's just moon dust, but that's another story."

Stink passed Mrs. Soso's house. "Hi, Stink," Mrs. Soso called. "What have you got there?"

"My new pet," said Stink. He held out Mr. McGoo for Mrs. Soso to see.

"Oh! I think I have a new pet growing on some cheese in the back of my fridge," Mrs. Soso joked.

"He's a *slime* mold," said Stink. "It's an organism."

"I see," said Mrs. Soso, but she did not look like she saw.

At the corner, Stink ran into Missy the dog walker. Missy the person was walking Missy the dog and a puppy named Anya.

"Hi, Missy!" said Stink. "I'm taking my new pet for a walk, too. And I don't even need a leash."

Missy the person peered at the blob in the dish. "That's your pet?"

"It's an organism," said Stink.

"Interesting," said Missy. But she did not look interested.

Missy the dog growled. Missy the dog tugged on her leash. Missy the dog stuck out her slobbery pink tongue and tried to lick the petri dish.

Missy the dog wanted to *eat* Stink's new pet. *Yikes!*

Stink held Mr. McGoo close. He crossed the street in a hurry, forgetting to wave good-bye. "Don't worry," Stink told Mr. McGoo. "I'll protect you from mean old slime-eating dogs."

Stink raced up the street to the pet store. Hello! It was Take a Picture With Your Pet Day at Fur & Fangs. Stink's lucky day!

Inside, Webster was getting his picture taken with a fat frog that had a big mouth and looked like Pac-Man.

"Hey! A Pac-Man frog!" said Stink. "Did you get a new pet, too?"

"It's my cousin's," said Webster. "I don't have a pet, so I'm borrowing Packy for the picture."

Sophie of the Elves was getting a photo taken with her pet hermit crab, Mr. Crab Cakes.

"Where's Toady?" asked Webster.

"Where's your guinea pig?" asked Sophie. "Didn't you bring Astro?"

"I brought my *new* pet," Stink told them, grinning.

"New pet!" said Sophie.

"New pet!" said Webster.

Stink held out Mr. McGoo proudly. He lifted the lid off of the shoe box. "Say hi to Mr. McGoo."

Sophie crinkled her forehead and wrinkled her nose. "So your new pet is a . . . slug?" she asked.

"So your new pet is a . . . booger?" asked Webster.

"Slime mold," said Stink. "It's an organism."

"Well, it looks like a giant booger," said Webster. He went to look for his cousin. Sophie scampered off to find a new shell for Mr. Crab Cakes.

"Say slime!" said Mrs. Birdwistle, the store's owner. She snapped a picture of Stink and Mr. McGoo.

When Stink got home, he taped the photo into his logbook. Stink and McGoo. Together. Forever.

* * *

The next day, Stink took his new pet to school. Things did not go much better.

"I brought my new pet today," Stink told his teacher. "I didn't want to leave him home alone, him being a new pet and all."

"Stink, you know we have rules about pets in our classroom," said Mrs. D.

"I know, but he's different. He's super quiet and polite. He's no trouble at all. And he hardly eats anything. You won't even know he's here. I promise."

Mrs. D. took one look at Mr. McGoo and pointed to the back of the classroom. "Put him in back by the tarantula. Just for today."

Stink set Mr. McGoo in back next to the guinea pig food, just to be safe.

Mrs. D. also let Stink sit in the back of the class for the day. While she talked

on about consonant blends, Stink
checked and rechecked his slime mold.
All the kids who walked by Mr. McGoo
said "Yuck" or "Ooh" or "Gross."

"Just ignore them," Riley said to
Stink.

CAPTAIN'S LOG: SLIMEDATE 3196.21
Not everybody appreciates science.
McGoo looking jittery.
Check back at 0900 hours.
Expect further difficulty.

"Slime molds are very scientific," Stink said, trying to convince them.

"Tell them they can solve mazes," said Riley. She nudged Stink with her elbow.

"Slime molds can solve mazes," said Stink. "Pretty smart for not having a brain, huh?"

"And they can power robots," Riley whispered to Stink.

"And did you know slime molds can power robots?" Stink said. "No lie."

Webster shrugged. Stink could tell Sophie didn't believe him. The other kids just stared.

"*And* they make good pets because they don't shed all over the place. They don't bark or bite or make loud noises."

But everybody seemed more interested in consonant blends than slime molds. Even though *slime mold* had not one but TWO consonant blends!

CAPTAIN'S LOG: SLIMEDATE 3196.22
Rough morning at school.
McGoo having trouble making friends.
Does not play well with others.

At lunch, nobody but Riley Rottenberger wanted to sit next to Stink and his slime mold. At recess, Webster made booger jokes. And in math class, Sophie said she was allergic to mold and moved to another pod.

During Not-So-Silent Reading, a kid pointed and said, "Hey! Your science project is getting out of its container."

"He's not my science—"

"He's attacking the guinea pig food," said another kid.

Maybe Mr. McGoo was a little bit hungry after all. Stink raised his hand and asked for a hall pass. He went straight to the cafeteria to ask the lunch lady for a Cheerio. He sure could use some cheery-o-ing up. But the lunch lady did not have a Cheerio.

All she had was Raisin Bran. Even a slime mold wouldn't eat boring old Raisin Bran.

When Stink got home from school, he took Mr. McGoo upstairs. Mr. McGoo looked a little raisiny—as wrinkled as a monkey ball. "I know you had a bad day at school," Stink said. "But look at the bright side. At least YOU don't have any homework."

CAPTAIN'S LOG: SLIMEDATE 3196.23
Mr. McGoo does _not_ like Raisin Bran.
Mr. McGoo does look like a raisin.

To cheer him up, Stink told Mr. McGoo, "Riley's coming over." Riley Rottenberger could be annoying, for sure, but at least she was a good partner in slime. In baby talk, Stink said, "Riley likes slime mold. Yes she does."

"Slime time!" Riley said when she got to Stink's house. Stink moved his light-up globe in closer so they could inspect their pets. "My slime mold is

way bigger than your slime mold," she said in a braggy voice.

"Don't listen to her, Mr. McGoo," whispered Stink.

"I like how you gave your slime mold a cool name," said Riley.

"Didn't you name yours?" asked Stink.

"Um," said Riley. "Sure. Its name is . . . um . . . Mrs. McGoo."

"Gross!" said Stink. "Our slime molds are not married."

"Fine. Then I'll change her name to Princess Slime Mold."

"How did you get Princess Slime Mold to grow so much?" Stink asked.

"Easy cheesy," said Riley. "I fed her. And you have to do stuff that makes her happy. Like they had us do for the animals at that farm we visited on our field trip."

Stink remembered. "Oh, yeah. We read books to the chickens and sang songs to the cows." So Stink and Riley sang "Twinkle, Twinkle, Little Slime" to Mr. McGoo and Princess Slime Mold. They read *Squish Squash Moo* till the cows came home.

Stink told a story about the time he got 21,280 jawbreakers in the mail *for free*. Stink told a joke. "What do molds, mucus, and big sisters have in common?"

"What?" asked Riley.

"They're all slime," said Stink. He laughed himself silly. "I bet Mr. McGoo will grow like crazy now."

"I think you're good to goo," said Riley. "I mean go." They started into fits of laughter all over again.

CAPTAIN'S LOG: SLIME DATE 3196.26
Attempt made to encourage further growth.
Mr. McGoo responds to singing. ♫ ♪
Ruler measurement indicates recent growth
at three centimeters!

"Don't forget to feed him." Riley unzipped her backpack. "I brought snacks!" She held up an apple and a bag of cheese doodles.

Stink took a bite of mealy apple while Riley ripped open the bag of munchy-crunchy cheese doodles. A wonderful waft of cheesy air puffed out of the bag. *Crunch-munch-crunch.*

"Cheese doodles sure are loud," said Stink.

"Yep," said Riley, munching.

"Cheese doodles sure smell milky and creamy," said Stink.

"Yep," said Riley, crunching.

"Cheese doodles sure turn your fin-gers electric orange," said Stink.

"The better to lick them off," said Riley, sucking the end of each finger.

She reached deep down into the bottom of the bag. As she pulled out a handful of cheese doodles, a small cloud of cheese dust poofed out of the bag.

"A-a-a-CHOO!" Riley sneezed a big sneeze. A giant sneeze. An elephant sneeze! Bits of electric orange gunk flew out of her mouth and landed smack-dab in the middle of Mr. McGoo.

Stink's mouth dropped open. He stared at his slime mold. "Gross!" he said. "Look what you did!"

"It's just cheese dust," said Riley. "What's the big deal?"

"You slimed my slime mold!" said Stink.

Riley peered at Mr. McGoo. "Stink, you can barely see it."

"You mean that neon-orange Mount Everest in the middle of Mr. McGoo?"

"I'm sure it won't hurt him," said Riley.

Stink squinted at her. "Let me see that bag," he said. He peered at the tiny words on the back. "Do you know what's in this stuff?"

Riley shrugged. "Um, cheese?"

Stink shook his head no. "Disodium phosphate, dextrose, artificial flavor, artificial color, disodium blah-blah, *more* disodium blah-blah. And don't forget corn syrup. Corn syrup sounds good but it is not."

"Sorry, Stink. Cheese dust makes me sneezy. But I'm sure it will be fine."

"Fine? An Unidentified Flying Sneeze just landed on Mr. McGoo. It's probably radioactive for all I know. *Anything* could happen now. How do you think the Glob became the Glob? What if Mr. McGoo morphs into a glob and takes over the planet?"

"That's only in the movies, Stink. Trust me. It's going to be fine."

"Stop saying 'fine.' It's *not* fine. Sneeze on your own slime mold." Stink could hear his voice coming out like a big meanie. As mean as Oogie Boogie. But he was so mad he didn't care.

"Fine," said Riley. She grabbed her slime mold and stomped down the stairs, leaving behind a trail of cheese dust. It no longer smelled milky and creamy.

It smelled like dog food.

It spelled doom.

CAPTAIN'S LOG: SLIMEDATE 3196.28
Cheese doodles not healthy for slime molds
and other living things.
Unidentified Flying Object landed
      in path of subject.
Origin ~~Un~~known: Riley Rottenberger.
Mr. McGoo in possible jeopardy.
      THAT MEANS TROUBLE.

Stink could not sleep three winks. Not two winks. Not one wink.

It was the Glob all over again. Ever since the Cheese Sneeze Incident of 1500 hours, Mr. McGoo had been acting strange.

CAPTAIN'S LOG: SLIMEDATE 3196.31
Strange Observation *1: McGoo turning odd color
SO#2: McGoo slimed cheese doodle crumb
SO#3 McGoo sent out three new tentacles
SO#4: McGoo crawling out of dish onto
light-up globe

Mr. McGoo *was* trying to take over the globe. The world!

Stink tried to sleep, but he kept thinking he felt something slippery and slimy crawling up his leg, his arm, wrapping around his throat. He tried counting sheep, but all he could see behind his eyelids were globs. Slimy, slime-mold globs.

What if his pet had turned into Frankenslime? A freak. A monster!

Stink grabbed his shark sleeping bag by its teeth. He tiptoed out and shut the door to his room behind him. He hightailed it over to Judy's room.

Judy was stretched out on her top bunk, folding gum wrappers to add to her gum-wrapper chain.

"Can I camp out in here tonight?" Stink asked Judy.

"Is it the Glob?" Judy asked. Stink

nodded. "You can have the bottom bunk," she said.

Stink frowned. "It's too close to the ground. Slime mold could climb right up and slime me in my sleep."

"I thought Mr. McGoo was your *pet*," said Judy.

"He is. Was. Until Rotten Riley went and sneezed radioactive disodium electric orange cheese dust on him and he morphed into . . . Frankenslime."

Stink checked under the bottom bunk. "There's already something green and blobby under the bed!"

"That's just my finger-knitting ball. I used glow-in-the-dark yarn."

"Okay." Stink climbed onto the bottom bunk and slipped into his sleeping bag for protection.

Judy turned off the overhead light but flicked on her flashlight pen so she could read.

Stink tried to close his eyes, but they blinked open in the shadowy dark. "Do you hear something?" he asked.

"Nope. But I'd *like* to hear you snoring. Go to sleep, Stink."

"But what if that is the homework-eating sound of Frankenslime? He could be eating my math problems right now."

"That was just me, turning the pages of my book."

"What if that sound is Frankenslime munching on my smelly sneakers?"

"Trust me, Stink. Nobody would be brave enough to go near those. Not even a Glob monster."

"What if that sound is the munch and crunch of Frankenslime devouring my race-car bed right this very minute? Then when he's done, he comes after me—"

"That was just me, chewing gum."

"Oh."

"It's eleven o'clock," Judy teased. "Do you know where your slime mold is?"

"Not funny. Frankenslime could ooze right across the hall and under your door and . . ." Stink hopped out of bed.

"Stink! Where are you going?" Judy asked.

He padded down the hall to the bathroom, shining his flashlight left and right into every dark corner. His heart thumped out of his chest as he passed his room. He tore off the lid of the hamper, grabbed a T-shirt, and raced back to Judy's room.

"Stink? What are you wearing?"

"Dad's T-shirt," said Stink.

"You risked your life so you could wear a sweaty old T-shirt that says 'Minnesota Is for Loons'? You must be loony tunes, Stink."

"Don't you get it? This will disguise my smell. Frankenslime won't know it's me. He'll think it's Dad and leave me alone." Stink got back into bed.

"Hey, why not spray on some of Mom's perfume, too, while you're at it?"

"Good idea," said Stink.

"I was joking," said Judy. "Can slime molds even smell?"

"How should I know?"

"I thought you were some kind of slime-mold expert or something," said Judy.

"Or something," said Stink. He hopped out of bed again and stretched a stuffed snake across the bottom of Judy's door. Then he climbed back into bed. "Do you think it's possible to sleep with one eye open?" he asked.

"Dolphins sleep with one eye open at a time," Judy told him.

Stink closed one eye. He took deep breaths. He counted sheep. Sharks. Skinks. Anything but blobs. Before you could say Frankenslime, his other eye started to close.

Frankenslime made himself as flat as a pancake and oozed under the door of Stink's room. He gurgled and burbled and bubbled his way across the hall. Glip. Glop. Gloop. Frankenslime hungry! Hungry for seven-year-old boy. A thick greenish drool dripped from the corners of the glob monster's slobbery, blobbery mouth. Help! Stink was going to be eaten alive!

Open wide and say . . .

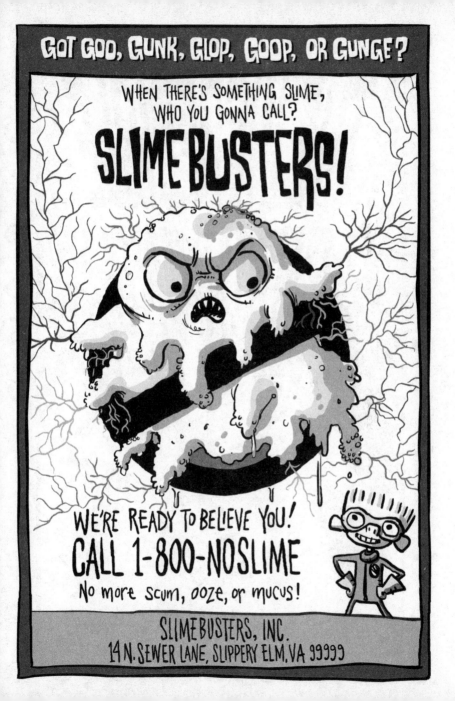

AARGH!"

Stink bolted awake from his nightmare. His heart was pounding. His neck was sweating. At least he was alive. *Phew.* He hadn't gotten Frankenslimed in his sleep.

Stink tiptoed across the hall to his room. He put his ear up to the door.

"Hear anything, Stinkerbell?" asked Judy, coming up behind him.

Stink shook his head no. "You try," he told Judy. She put her ear to the door.

"Hear any slurping sounds? Sucking sounds? Swallowing sounds?"

"Nothing," said Judy. "Slurp factor zero. All quiet on the glob front."

"What if it's quiet because every-thing in my whole room is eaten?" said Stink. "Poor Toady. And Astro."

"You mean you left your pets in there?" asked Judy.

"Hey, I was busy trying to save *myself,*" said Stink.

Judy put her hand on the knob. "You're going to have to go in there sometime," she said.

"Wait." Stink came back wearing a rain slicker and rubber boots. He put on goggles. "This is my hazmat suit." He held the inside of his elbow over his mouth. "I'm going in."

Slowly, Stink opened the door a crack. *Creeeeak!*

"P.U. What's that smell?" Judy asked, waving a hand in front of her nose.

"Told you," said Stink, shutting the door. "My room is slimed. Blobbed. Globbed. That smell is radioactive cheese dust that ballooned up into a mushroom cloud of stink."

"Just open the door, Stink." Judy pinched her nose shut.

Stink opened the door at last.

The room was not slimed. The room was not filled with radioactive cheese dust.

Judy looked around. "I think you're safe, Stink. The awful smell is just boy feet," she said, pointing to Stink's sneakers.

Stink rushed over to Mr. McGoo. Something *was* wrong. *Way* wrong.

Mr. McGoo looked pale. Mr. McGoo looked sickly. Mr. McGoo looked like a hundred-year-old shrunken head.

"He looks like a Shrinky Dink!" cried Stink.

"The incredible shrinking slime," said Judy.

Instead of growing by leaps and blobs in a single night, Mr. McGoo had shrunk.

CAPTAIN'S LOG: SLIMEDATE 3196.37
Return to SOTC (Scene of the Crime.)
Patient in weak state. CAUSE UNKNOWN.
Radioactive cheese doodle sneeze suspected.

"Maybe he has Slime Mold Flu or something," said Judy.

"More like Cheezy Doodles Flu," said Stink.

"I think Mr. McGoo threw up," said Judy.

"He didn't throw up. He just *looks* like throw-up."

"Or maybe the smell of your stinky sneakers finally did him in," said Judy.

"Not funny," said Stink. "This is an emergency."

"Maybe he's hungry. Go back downstairs and bring me three oat flakes and a pancake."

When Stink got back, Judy fed Mr. McGoo the three oat flakes. "So what's the pancake for?" Stink asked.

"Me," said Judy, taking a bite. She

set it down on the desk. "Stink, I know what to do. Go to my room and get my doctor kit."

Stink got Judy's way-official kit. Judy took out her stethoscope. She held it up to Mr. McGoo.

"I do not detect a heartbeat," said Dr. Judy.

"Do you hear *anything*?" asked Stink.

"Just you breathing down my neck," said Judy. Next she took Mr. McGoo's temperature.

"Is it normal?" asked Stink.

"What's normal for a slime mold?" Judy frowned.

CAPTAIN'S LOG: SLIMEDATE 3196.41
Slime mold reported to sick bay.
Dr. Judy Moody taking over command.
Air temperature indoors: 68 degrees.
Slime mold temperature: zero and dropping.
No HEARTBEAT. Keep eye out for rapid change in temperature.
CONDITION: CRITICAL.

"Stinker. Get me a blanket," said Judy.

Stink pulled the covers off his race-car bed. Judy bundled the blanket all around Mr. McGoo's dish like a nest.

"Now get me a lamp."

Stink moved the light-up globe closer.

"Now I need some warm rocks," said Judy. "Stat."

"Warm rocks? What am I, your gofer?"

"Do you want Mr. McGoo to get better or not?" Judy asked. Stink nodded.

"Then stat!" Judy repeated. "And that, if you don't know, means quick, hurry, now-not-yesterday."

Stink raced outside and collected the first five rocks he saw. "Here. I heated them up under the hot water just in case."

"Perfect," said Judy. She carefully placed the rocks on the blanket nest around Mr. McGoo. "We want his environment to be nice and warm so he'll bounce back and have a full recovery.

"Now go get the mister," Judy ordered.

"Mister who?"

"Not Mister who. The mister thingy Dad uses to spray plants."

Stink went downstairs and brought back the mister. Judy spritzed Mr. McGoo with a fine mist. "To make sure he doesn't dry out."

"Maybe we should give him some baby aspirin," said Stink.

"Good thinking," said Judy. "I have some in my doctor kit." She took out a tiny plastic container and shook it in front of Stink.

"That's not baby aspirin. Those are Tic Tacs."

"No, get me four pencils," said Judy.

Stink got one-two-three-four pencils.

Judy laid the pencils out on the desk—two up and down and two across, making a tic-tac-toe board.

"Since we have to wait, we can play tic-tac-toe with Tic Tacs. You can be the red Tic Tacs and I'll be green."

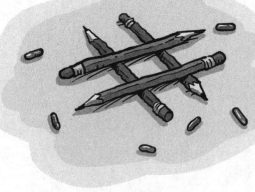

"I want to be green."

"Good," said Judy. "Because I secretly wanted to be red."

✳ ✳ ✳

After two pancakes each and ten games of Tic Tac tic-tac-toe, Mr. McGoo started to look like himself again. "It's working!" said Stink. "You did it. Dr. Judy, you could cure a rainy day. Just like Dr. McCoy in *Star Trek*. Thanks!"

"I'll send you my bill in the morning," said Dr. Judy.

"What's it going to cost me?" asked Stink.

"Let's see. How about one blue-raspberry Jolly Rancher, ten gum wrappers, and your fortune-cookie eraser."

"Aw, that's my best one!"

"With a fortune, of course," said Judy. "And you better make it a good one."

Stink knew just what to write.

SOON YOU WILL HAVE THE SLIME OF YOUR LIFE!

McGoo's Log

McGOO'S LOG   STINKDATE 229.1

HUMANOID ATE BOWL OF CEREAL.
ONLY GAVE ME <u>ONE</u> OAT.
MR. STINGY!

McGOO'S LOG   STINKDATE 229.2

HUMANOID STARING AT ME. HOW RUDE!
HELP — BRIGHT LIGHT!
<u>STOP</u> POKING ME. CUT IT OUT. THAT TICKLES!

McGOO'S LOG   STINKDATE 229.4

HUMANOID #1 MAKING STRANGE
NOISES WITH HUMANOID #2.

APPEARS TO BE SOME KIND
OF COMMUNIQUÉ!

#2

#1

#3   #1   McGOO'S LOG   STINKDATE 229.6

TRIED TO MAKE CONTACT WITH
HUMANOID #1. NO RESPONSE.

TOO BUSY EATING CHEEZY DOODLES
WITH HUMANOID #3.

CHEEZY DOODLE

Over the next few days, Mr. McGoo grew by lumps and bounds, faster than ever. Warp speed!

Stink built a maze out of Snappos. By the next afternoon, Mr. McGoo had slimed his way through the whole entire maze. Stink showed his friends. "Slime molds find the shortest route through a maze. It's a scientific fact. No lie."

Even Webster and Sophie of the Elves, his anti-slime friends, had to admit it was way cool.

"Good boy," Stink cooed to Mr. McGoo. "Who says you don't have a brain?"

"We still think it's weird to talk baby talk to slime," said Webster.

"We still think we'd like your new pet better if it was a sugar glider," said Sophie.

* * *

Mr. McGoo slimed the oat flakes that Stink fed him. He slimed the grains of rice. He slimed the macaroni elbow.

Spores must have landed all over the place, because slime mold was growing on everything. On the desk where sticky maple syrup had dripped from Judy's pancake. Up and down Astro's guinea pig tunnel. On top of Stink's math book. Mr. McGoo had taken over all of Africa on the globe. Not to mention Asia and part of Antarctica.

He even slimed the juice box Stink left on his desk. One day it looked like a box of juice. The next day it looked like brains.

CAPTAIN'S LOG: SLIMEDATE 3196.48

Alarming Observation #1: SLIME MOLD OUT OF CONTROL!

AO#2: Spores must have spread when Dr. Judy misted Mr. McGoo. SON OF SLIME!

AO#3: Juice box left unattended.

AO#4: Mom and Dad found McGoo-slimed juice box. Violation noted. Action taken.

Mom and Dad did N-O-T want mold growing in the house. They insisted that Stink move Mr. McGoo outside. He looked around for just the right spot: someplace warm and damp with room to grow.

111

The kiddie swimming pool!

Perfect. Stink scrubbed out all the yucky leaves and gunk. He set his slime mold in the bottom of the now-clean pool. Next he covered the pool with an old tablecloth, like a blanket. Then Stink wrapped a real blanket around himself, took out his flashlight, sat in a lawn chair, and started reading a book to Mr. McGoo.

"*All day long he hears squish squash moo . . .*"

"Stink!" Judy called from the back door. "Dad says you have to come inside now."

"But I'm camping out," said Stink. "I'm having a sleepover with Mr. McGoo. I mean a *slime*over." Stink couldn't help cracking up.

Judy went inside for a minute and came back. "Mom says no sleepover tonight."

"It's a *slime*over," said Stink.

"No slimeover, either. Too cold."

Stink lifted a corner of the tablecloth.

"Night, night. Sleep tight. Don't let the bedbugs bite," he whispered to Mr. McGoo. Then Stink headed inside, dragging his blanket behind him.

Stink called Riley and told her all about the Juice Box Incident of 1500 hours. He told her all about having to keep Mr. McGoo outside, and he told her that he wasn't allowed to have a slimeover.

"Don't worry," Riley said. "Tons of slime molds grow outside. Hey, you want to build a slime house tomorrow? You know, like a dog house, but for slime."

"A dog-vomit house," said Stink, cracking himself up. "Cool! But you have to promise, no cheese-sneezing."

"Cross my heart and hope to slime," said Riley.

Upstairs in his room, Stink curled up in the window seat and gazed out at Mr. McGoo until he fell asleep.

✴ ✴ ✴

Brring! Ding-ding-ding! Stink woke up. What was that noise? Doorbell! He peeked out the window to see who was at the front door.

Riley Rottenberger!

Stink opened the door. "What are you doing here?"

Riley pointed to Stink's sticky-up hair. "Ha, ha! Bed head!"

"What time is it, anyway?" asked Stink.

"Time to start building a slime house!" said Riley, holding up a pink hammer.

Slime house? Mr. McGoo! Stink had almost forgotten about him! He ran out to the kiddie pool in his pajamas and bare feet. Riley hurried after him.

Holy elbow macaroni!

There was no tablecloth over the kiddie pool anymore! Stink peered inside.

No. Way. No. How. Mr. McGoo was G-O-N-E *gone.*

Stink turned to Riley in a panic. "Where could he be? He was right here. I put him here myself. I covered him with a tablecloth to stay warm."

"Slime molds can crawl, you know," said Riley. "Maybe he got lonely and joined up with some other slime molds and they all crawled away like one big slime sausage."

Stink looked under the deck. He looked beneath the old swing set. He looked in the sandbox. Mr. McGoo

was nowhere to be found. The slime
sausage was nowhere. . . .

"What if Bigfoot came
through here last night and
thought Mr. McGoo was pea-
nut butter . . . and ate him?"
Riley rolled her eyes.

"Or what if aliens landed in
the backyard and thought he
was an alien life-form and
took him back to outer space?"
Riley rolled her eyes again.

"*Or*, what if a meteorite fell on him
and—"

"Get real, Stink," said Riley. All of a

sudden Riley pointed up at a tree. In the branches. A tablecloth!

"Or," she said, "what if the wind blew off the tablecloth, Mr. McGoo got too cold, and he shriveled up to nothing and disappeared?"

"That, too," said Stink with a sigh.

CAPTAIN'S LOG: SLIMEDATE 3196.52

UNBELIEVABLE OBSERVATION #1:
    MR. McGOO GONE FOR REAL!

UO#2: seems impossible but there it is.
UO#3: Stink and Riley mourn his passing.

Stink felt sad. Like the time he buried his goldfish under the rosebush. And the time his millipede croaked. This time around, he couldn't even have a slime-mold funeral.

"Mr. McGoo was the best," said Stink.

"He was the best dog vomit around," Riley agreed.

"Remember when Mrs. Soso thought he was refrigerator mold?"

"No," said Riley.

"Remember when Missy the dog almost ate him?"

"Nope," said Riley.

"Remember when I got scared and thought he was Frankenslime?"

"Nuh-uh," said Riley. "Sorry. Wasn't there."

"Remember when we read to him and sang 'Twinkle, Twinkle, Little Slime'?"

"That I remember!" said Riley.

"We should have a moment of silence," said Stink.

Stink and Riley stood silently, gazing at the kiddie pool, remembering for a moment all the fun times they'd had with Mr. McGoo.

"You could always grow another slime mold," said Riley.

Stink shook his head. "It wouldn't be the same."

"You can come to my house to visit Princess Slime Mold anytime," said Riley.

"Thanks," said Stink. "Can you help me put the pool back in the shed?"

"Sure," said Riley. They each grabbed an end and dragged it across the yard to the toolshed.

"Want to stay for pancakes?" asked Stink. "My dad makes killer silver-dollar pancakes. Mr. McGoo loved them."

"Why not?" asked Riley.

On the way back inside, Stink noticed something about the grass where the kiddie pool had been. "Hey, look! I think maybe it's a crop circle! Or a fairy ring! Wait till I tell Sophie of the Elves!"

"The grass is just smooshed from where the kiddie pool was sitting," said Riley.

"I don't know," said Stink, looking a little closer.

"What's this?" he asked, pointing to a jellylike lump of goo in the grass.

Riley took a look. "Is it an . . . organism?"

"An organism from outer space!" said Stink.

"Outer space slime!" said Riley.

"No, wait," said Stink. "I bet it's a silver-dollar pancake . . . from Mars! A Martian pancake!"

"That's no pancake, Stink. Not even Martians would eat that," said Riley. "It looks more like an inside-out frog. Frog guts! Cool!"

"It's too big for frog guts. Maybe it's the guts of a *giant* amphibian, like some prehistoric tetrapod or something."

Stink studied the new goo some more. It looked like . . . an alien booger. It looked like an alien jellyfish. It looked like . . .

Wait just an outer-space second! Stink had an idea. Might it be, *could* it be? Now he knelt down, leaned over, and took a super sniff with his super sniffer. The goo smelled like rotten eggs, all right. *Eureka!*

"I think I know what it is," said Stink in awe. He could barely breathe the words. "I think it's star jelly."

"Star jelly?" whispered Riley.

"Star jelly is like a blob of slime

that's left after a meteor shower," said Stink. "It's way rare."

"Really?" asked Riley.

"No lie," said Stink. "Just think. Alien star jelly right here in my very own backyard."

"Wow," said Riley in a hushed voice.

Stink put his face right up to the new blob of goo.

"Riley," he said. "Say hello to Mr. McGoo Two!"

Megan McDonald

is the author of the popular Judy Moody and Stink series. She says, "Once, while I was visiting a class, the kids chanted, 'Stink! Stink! Stink!' as I entered the room. In that moment, I knew that Stink had to have a series all his own." Megan McDonald lives in California.

Peter H. Reynolds

is the illustrator of all the Judy Moody and Stink books. He says, "Stink reminds me of myself growing up: dealing with a sister prone to teasing and bossing around—and having to get creative in order to stand tall beside her." Peter H. Reynolds lives in Massachusetts.

BE SURE TO CHECK OUT ALL OF STINK'S ADVENTURES!

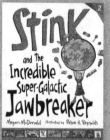

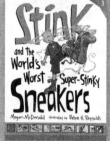

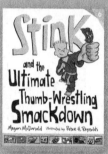

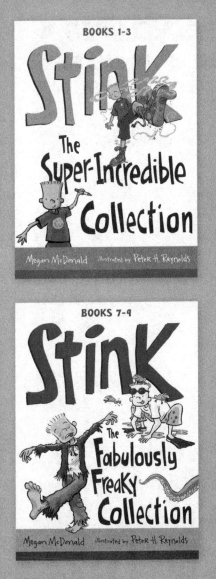

JUMP-START YOUR STINK COLLECTION WITH A BOXED SET OFFERING A TRIO OF PAPERBACK TITLES:

STINK,
THE WALKING ENCYCLOPEDIA,
HAS COLLECTED SOME OF HIS FAVORITE FREAKY FACTS INTO THREE COOL VOLUMES.

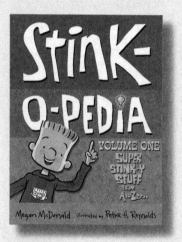

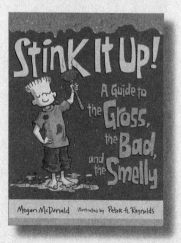

STINK

has a new and improved website!

www.stinkmoody.com

Go online to:

- Access exclusive top secret content.

- Throw a big Stink birthday bash!

- Make your own comics.

- Learn more about slime mold!

- Read passages that never made it into the final books.

- Find lots of Stink-y information and activities!